MW00592929

This journal belongs to

____

____

From the book *Barefoot in Paris* by
Ina Garten, published by Clarkson
Potter/Publishers.

Potter Style
Printed in China
www.clarksonpotter.com
ISBN: 1-4000-5393-5

The first part of this journal is designed to be used as an address book to keep track of your favorite bistros, cafés, and shops. Use the rest of the journal to jot down a favorite recipe or record a favorite meal or wine recommendation. The rest of it is up to you.

Bakeries

Bistros

Cafés

Cheese Shops

Farmer's Markets

Wine

recipe for ______

from the kitchen of ______

makes ______

recipe for ______________________________

from the kitchen of ______________________

makes ___________________________________

recipe for

from the kitchen of

makes

recipe for ______

from the kitchen of ______

makes ______

recipe for ______

from the kitchen of ______

makes ______

recipe for ______________________________

from the kitchen of ______________________________

makes ______________________________

recipe for

from the kitchen of

makes

recipe for ______________________________

from the kitchen of ______________________________

makes ______________________________

recipe for ______________________________

from the kitchen of ______________________________

makes ______________________________

recipe for ______________________________

from the kitchen of ______________________________

makes ______________________________

recipe for ______________________________

from the kitchen of ______________________________

makes ______________________________

LUCIEN
LEGRAND
filles &

LUCIEN
LEGRAND
filles &